PIRATES of the CARIBBEAN
JACK SPARROW

Silver

by Rob Kidd
Illustrated by Jean-Paul Orpinas

Based on the earlier life of the character, Jack Sparrow,
created for the theatrical motion picture,
"Pirates of the Caribbean: The Curse of the Black Pearl"
Screen Story by Ted Elliott & Terry Rossio and Stuart Beattie and Jay Wolpert,
Screenplay by Ted Elliott & Terry Rossio,
and characters created for the theatrical motion pictures
"Pirates of the Caribbean: Dead Man's Chest" and
"Pirates of the Caribbean: At World's End"
written by Ted Elliott & Terry Rossio

visit us at www.abdopublishing.com

Reinforced library bound edition published in 2009 by Spotlight, a division of ABDO Publishing Group, 8000 West 78th Street, Edina, Minnesota 55439. This edition reprinted by arrangement with Hyperion Books for Children, an imprint of Disney Book Group, LLC. www.disneybooks.com

Special thanks to Ken Becker, Elizabeth Braswell, and Rich Thomas.

Library of Congress Cataloging-in-Publication Data

Kidd, Rob.
 Pirates of the Caribbean, Jack Sparrow / by Rob Kidd ; illustrated by Jean-Paul Orpinas. -- Reinforced library bound ed.
   v. cm.
 "Based on the earlier life of the character, Jack Sparrow, created for the theatrical motion picture, 'Pirates of the Caribbean: The Curse of the Black Pearl'. . . and characters created for the theatrical motion pictures 'Pirates of the Caribbean: Dead Man's Chest' and 'Pirates of the Caribbean 3.'"
 Contents: The coming storm -- The siren song -- The pirate chase -- The sword of Cortés -- The Age of Bronze -- Silver -- City of gold -- The timekeeper.
 ISBN 978-1-59961-528-8 (book 6: Silver)
 I. Orpinas, Jean-Paul, ill. II. Pirates of the Caribbean, the curse of the Black Pearl (Motion picture) III. Pirates of the Caribbean, dead man's chest (Motion picture) IV. Pirates of the Caribbean, at world's end (Motion picture) V. Title.
 PZ7.K53148Pir 2008
 [Fic]--dc22

                                                                    2008000720

Silver

CHAPTER ONE

$\mathcal{I}$t should have been the *end* of his latest grand adventure. But things were never easy for Jack Sparrow, the wily teenaged captain of the mighty *Barnacle*.

Jack fumed. Wasn't he—and his crew—entitled to a little rest and relaxation? They had definitely earned it. After a precious item—the Sun-and-Stars medallion—was stolen from the native village of one of Jack's sailors, named Tumen, the crew of the *Barnacle* went and got it back. Just like they

1

said they would. Along the way, they'd had a showdown with a notorious black-arts practitioner, Madame Minuit. And defeated a whole bunch of possessed partygoers. And added another member to their crew. Oh, yes, *and* accidentally turned the entire city of New Orleans into bronze.

And now they *should have* been sailing back to the Yucatán with the horrible medallion that turned everything into bronze—including Jack's tooth. Instead, they had been stopped by a pirate ship. And not just any pirate ship. One captained by a lady—and not just any lady. The *mother* of Jack's first mate, Arabella. Who was supposed to be *dead*. And Mom—otherwise known as Captain Laura Smith—had a first mate. And it wasn't just *any* first mate, either. It was the feared pirate Left-Foot Louis.

In other words, it was all bad.

And very, very confusing.

Most of all for Arabella.

"I thought ye were dead," she said quietly, staring at her long-lost mother.

"Oh. Well, I wasn't," Arabella's mother, the pirate captain Laura Smith, responded.

Arabella didn't know what to say. The last memories she had of her mother were of her being dragged out of her family's pub—the Faithful Bride—by Left-Foot Louis. People dragged anywhere by pirates usually didn't show up again. Ever.

Arabella was shocked to see her mom alive—and also confused. *And* a little angry. She grew up serving pirates their ale while her dad passed out in his drink every night. All without the comfort or wisdom of a mother. And now here was her mom, suddenly back in her life again. Alive and captain of her own ship. Wanting to make nice like everything was all right again. Just like that.

Arabella opened and closed her mouth several times, trying to think of something to say, and failing—something she was completely unused to.

"A-*hem*!" Jack said, sidling up to Arabella, hands clasped casually behind his back. For once she was grateful for his interruptions. "Just a reminder here, mates. As captain of this here vessel, all extravessel communications—that is, from us to you, 'Mommy'— must be authorized, sanctioned, and *made* by me. No members of either crew are to engage in communication except through the captain. Which is me. Because . . . well, there doesn't need to be a 'because.' That's just the way things is."

"Arabella," Captain Smith said, completely ignoring Jack. The pirate bit her lip—almost exactly like a certain first mate aboard the *Barnacle*, Jack noticed. She was having a hard time fighting the emotions that were threatening to overwhelm her.

Apparently, motherly annoyance won out.

"Arabella!" her mother said again, now with a sternness in her voice and a frown on her face. "What are you doing on a *boat* . . . a barely seaworthy one at that . . ."

"Hey!" Jack protested, offended on behalf of the mighty *Barnacle*.

". . . in the middle of the Gulf of Mexico with . . . sailors who are barely older than *boys* . . ."

"Hey!" Jean, Tumen, and Tim, all crew members, said, also offended.

"And a bloody *aristocrat* . . ." Captain Smith continued.

"And what is wrong with aristocracy?" Fitzwilliam demanded.

"... a mangy catlike thing ..."

Constance, the *Barnacle's* resident girl-turned-cat, hissed at this insult.

"... and a captain who is clearly mad?"

"Well, thank you, ma'm," Jack said smiling.

Arabella found her own voice. "I might ask *you*, mother," she said indignantly, "what *ye* are doing *alive*?!"

"Whoever said I was *dead*, dear?" Captain Smith retorted.

"Oh, yes, it was *crazy* for me to think ye were dead all these years," Arabella snapped back, putting her hands on her hips. The tone in her voice made the rest of the *Barnacle's* crew wince, just as it had countless pirates she had put in their place over the years at the Faithful Bride. "Considering you were forcibly taken out of my life by a *pirate* ... and didn't so much as send a card or letter saying you were sailing the high seas, having the time of your life!"

"And *ye!*" Arabella continued, turning to Left-Foot Louis, pointing both her finger and her rage at him. "*Ye* knew me mum were alive all along and didn't see fit to tell me. All that time. Even when I was about to *kill* ye!"*

"It's implied in the code, love," Left-Foot Louis grumbled. "A pirate never gives away another."

"A pirate never gives away a *mother*?" Jack asked, misunderstanding and squinting in confusion. Louis and Captain Smith just looked at one another, confused.

Arabella bit her lip. She wanted to hit something. She felt like crying but didn't want to break down in front of everyone.

---

* This piratical exchange between Arabella and Louis took place in Vol. 3, *The Pirate Chase*

And all these years, she had thought that Louis had *killed* her mother!

"Pull up alongside us and drop anchor," Captain Smith ordered the crew of the *Barnacle.* "You all can come aboard and we'll talk this out."

"Well, how about *no . . .*" Jack said.

"*What?*" Captain Smith demanded, outraged. It was obvious she wasn't used to being talked to in such a manner. She flipped her auburn hair over her shoulder. She looked so much like Arabella it was a little creepy.

"We're not about to get cozy with a bunch of *pirates*," Jack spat. "Even if some of said pirates are related to some perfectly good first mates and sailors. You're—still— *pirates.*"

Arabella gave him a thankful look.

"I don't want to come aboard. Not until I have some time to think about things,"

Arabella told her mother, setting her jaw defiantly.

Fitzwilliam stepped up next to Arabella. But if she thought he was coming to her support, she was badly mistaken.

"Arabella," Fitzwilliam began, "Laura—er, *Captain* Laura Smith is your *mother*," he admonished her. He took the tone of a particularly annoying, know-it-all big brother. Arabella bristled. "And one really must obey one's parents. It is the proper thing to do."

"Oh, yes, just like ye *properly* obeyed yer dad and stayed on the family plantation to marry a rich girl and raise bananas, aye?" Arabella said sarcastically.

Tim Hawk, the *Barnacle*'s newest crew member piped up. "Actually, the whole 'armed pirates and shiny cannons' thing weighs this situation in their favor. I'll go over."

"Do what ye will. I'm still *not* going over," Arabella said stubbornly.

"That's right. She's not. Because *I* order her not to," Jack added, just as stubbornly. "And none of you is going either," Jack said pointedly to Fitz and Tim.

Tumen looked at Jean and sighed. "Whatever," he said bravely but a little tiredly. It was going to come to a fight no matter what. And it was all going to delay him going back home, returning the medallion, and clearing his name.

"*Fine*," Captain Smith said with a strange smile. "If you won't come to us, we'll simply need to bring you over ourselves."

Jack smirked, hand to his now-bronze cutlass.* A chance to fight with real pirates! This was an opportunity he had

* Jack's sword was turned to bronze in our previous adventure, Vol. 5, the *Age of Bronze*

been waiting for for a long time. . . .

But Captain Laura Smith didn't order the cannons readied or muskets loaded. She even sheathed her own sword. "Mr. Silverback," she called out. A squat, smart-looking sailor with a prosthetic—well, peg—leg came hobbling forward. His clothes were in slightly better condition than the rest of the crew's, and his smile was definitely superior. That wasn't what drew stares from the crew of the *Barnacle*, however. It was the peg leg.

It was made of pure crystal. Sunlight danced over it and cast bright reflections all over the decks of both ships.

Tim Hawk gasped in horror and recognition.

"I agree, the crystal leg thing's tacky, lad," Jack said, looking at his newest crew member curiously. "But not the *ugliest* thing I've seen on the high seas."

"Please, invite our guests over," Captain Smith said, grinning.

"Would be nothin' but my pleasure, Captain," Silverback said, smiling nastily back.

He held his hand out towards the *Barnacle*. Not sure what the pirate with the weird leg was doing, but getting a general 'threatening' feel from the gesture, Jack moved in front of Arabella, protecting her. Normally he would never dare to do such a thing, but her mother looked pretty determined—and a mad mother is not someone you want to play around with.

With a quick sweep of Silverback's hand, Jack and his crew felt a tingling in their limbs. Then they disappeared.

CHAPTER TWO

A moment later, the six crewmates—and the cat—found themselves dizzy and disoriented.

And no longer on the *Barnacle*.

Jack looked around, confused by the sudden shift in perspective. They were higher up off the sea. And aboard a different deck. And surrounded by a number of pirates.

They had somehow been transported to the other ship!

Jack groped for his sword. Whatever

magic was used, the effect was extremely disorienting. No one else was doing any better—Fitzwilliam was staggering around, trying to keep from falling.

The pirate Silverback's crystal leg was flashing a clear, sky blue, which wasn't helping the situation any. It gave Jack a headache. The sailor smiled nastily at him . . . and revealed a matching crystal tooth. Which also flashed blue.

"I have one of those," Jack said with interest, pointing at his recently bronzed incisor* Of course, it's not as fancy as yours. It's just metal, and it doesn't blink and kidnap perfectly innocent adventurers. . . ."

"Now, who do we have here, Mr. Silverback?" Captain Smith inquired, once again ignoring Jack. She grinned smugly.

---

*Jack's tooth was turned to bronze in our previous volume, *The Age of Bronze*.

Kind of like Arabella when she was going on about some subject that no one else knew anything about.

"Well," the crystal-legged pirate began with relish. He leaned on a cane—which had a crystal pommel—and hobbled back and forth in front of the crew, lecturing like a school-teacher. He spoke very clearly and snootily, not like a normal pirate in sea-slang. "I recognize one of the *lads*—a fellow by the name of Tim Hawk, whom I've encountered before."

The crew of the *Barnacle* turned and looked questioningly at their newest addition. Tim shook his head, scared. This obviously wasn't the best time to tell his side of the story.

"Of course, your daughter, Arabella Smith," Silverback continued, waving his hand in the air. "Tortugan barmaid formerly of the *Faithful Bride*. Finally reunited with her loving mother." He smiled in what was probably supposed to be an approving fashion, but it came out sickly. "For the others I am going to need some help."

Silverback closed his eyes tightly. His hand fell down and brushed his crystal leg. His lip lifted a little in concentration, and the crew of the *Barnacle* could see that his tooth now flashed yellow. The light danced off the pommel on his cane in a rhythmic, hypnotic fashion. His leg also began to pulse eerily, with the same yellow light.

"Ah, yes . . . your young captain, *Jack Sparrow*, also recently of Tortuga."

Jack jumped involuntarily. Silverback's eyes were still closed, but he pointed directly at the captain of the *Barnacle*. It was creepy. Somehow far creepier than all the weird mystics and things back in New Orleans. What else could he find out about Jack?

Not the *whole* truth, he hoped. . . .

". . . and also briefly in possession of the fabled Sword of Cortés," the pirate continued.

Left-Foot Louis snarled. Jack stuck his tongue out at him.

Silverback continued, ignoring both of them.

"Fitzwilliam P. Dalton the Third, runaway heir to the Dalton fortune. Such a pretty boy—and worth just as pretty a *ransom*, I'd wager."

The aristocrat snarled defiantly.

"I don't suppose you can figure out his middle name?" Jack asked hopefully. "It's been stumpin' us."

Silverback ignored Jack, then continued

". . . and Tumen, a . . . *Mayan* sailor. Well, well," Silverback gave the boy a once-over. Tumen glared steadily back. "And last but not least, Creole sailor Jean Magliore and his sister, Constance. Who is currently serving time as a cat—having been a victim of a spell cast by Tia Dalma."

Constance yowled and leapt into Jean's arms. "Well, at least *someone* knows the truth about you," Jean whispered into his sister's ear, stroking her back.*

Louis growled, rubbing the three scars on his face that were left there by Constance.** It was a constant reminder that he had faced Jean, Tumen and Constance a few times before. "You three! I shoulda killed ye when I had the chance!" He stomped his foot and lunged forward. He didn't even bother going for his sword, much preferring to take them out with his bare hands. And he could. Louis was a huge, hulking pirate.

---

*Jean has had a very hard time convincing his crewmates that his sister is actually a cat!

**As recounted in Vol. 2, *The Siren Song*

"Stop!" Captain Smith commanded. "You're no longer aboard—or *captain*—of the *Cutlass*, Louis. May I remind you. You are a member of the *crew* of *Fleur de la Mort*. *My* ship. And you will do as I say."

"*Fleur de la Mort?*" Jack whispered to Jean, wondering exactly how the ship's name translated.

"'Flower of death,'" Jean whispered back, inching away from Louis.

"Cheery," Jack muttered.

"I *know* I'm no longer a captain," Louis said with a petulant whine, just like a little kid. "Ye don't have to keep reminding me."

"Apparently I do," Arabella's mother retorted—just like a mother. "Now, what do you say to our guests?"

Louis looked down at his feet, kicking one left foot miserably against the other.

"i'm sorry" he said, so quietly it could barely be heard above the creaking of the ship and crash of waves.

"What was that?" Captain Laura Smith prodded, cupping her hand to her ear.

"I SAID, I'M SORRY!" he roared. Jack put his hand to his bandana, to keep it from flying off with the force of the pirate's breath. Which wasn't very fresh, we might add.

"That's very good," Captain Smith said soothingly.

"I wouldn't be here on your ship serving you, if it weren't for your little *brat*," Louis continued, not willing to let go of the last word. "It was she who held the all powerful Sword of Cortés in her hands and said 'May my mother find you. May justice be done, and may it be done by *her* hand,'* and now,

* In Vol. 3, *The Pirate Chase*

21

here I am" the vicious pirate put his head in his hands, frustrated.

"Perhaps Mr. Left-Foot needs a bit more *encouragement* to behave," Silverback suggested. He sidled as gracefully as he could—considering his leg—up to Captain Smith's side and rubbed his hands smarmily. "Perhaps you should lock Louis belowdecks, while he thinks about what he did. Or some other punishment that he's likely to understand. Hang him off the railing, perhaps? Make him walk the plank, maybe?"

It was obvious that Silverback had no love for the dread pirate Louis. Jack thought about how he could use that. There was that old saying: 'any enemy of my enemy is a friend of mine. . . .' But there was something *particularly* unsavory about Silverback. And not just how he could make people magically disappear and reappear somewhere else.

He looked untrustworthy, even for a pirate.

"Give me a plain old tough-guy scallywag any day," Jack muttered.

"Silverback does not look very trustworthy, does he?" Fitzwilliam whispered in agreement. "I have seen many others like him. Fancy clothes, snooty appearance, and such. All vile underneath," Fitzwilliam continued, before glancing down at his own silk suit and checking himself.

"All *that* brute understands is the lock and key. And the whip," Silverback went on.

This time Louis *did* draw his sword. With a wordless bellow of rage he raised it and lunged at Silverback. The smarmy sailor didn't budge an inch. Instead, he calmly raised a hand and pointed at Louis. His crystal leg glowed an angry, fiery red. Left-Foot Louis's sword flew from his grasp as if it were knocked by an invisible hand. It landed on the deck with a sharp *clang*, embedding itself in a plank. The other pirates stepped back.

Left-Foot Louis howled and pulled out his knife, gripping it strongly with both hands. Silverback raised his hand again.

"That's enough!" Captain Smith roared. She strode between them, hands on her hips. "I'm running a pirate ship here, not a gladiator arena. *Both* of you go belowdecks until you've calmed down for a while. Mr. Reece?"

A cleaner-than-usual pirate came forward. He was handsome, with clear blue eyes and a smart red bandana, and he responded with almost military precision. "Please escort them down the hatch—and don't let them up for at least three hours," Captain Smith said.

"Aye, ma'am," Mr. Reece replied with a grin. At least three of his teeth sparkled gold. But they were set in an otherwise perfect row of pearly whites, and looked more dashing than dastardly.

"I'm beginning to feel a lot less special," Jack said, touching his own bronze tooth. "It seems like these days *everyone* has one of these."

While Mr. Reece led Silverback and Louis away, Captain Smith began ordering the rest of her crew about.

"You and you! Make fast the *Barnacle* to the *Fleur*. We'll tow her for now, until we figure out what to do with her. Pull up the anchor and hoist the sails. We're moving out, lads!" She gave Arabella a stern look. "And we're taking you and your crew with us, young lady. Whether you like it or not."

CHAPTER THREE

$\mathcal{T}$he crew of the *Barnacle* watched glumly as their little boat was tied up behind the *Fleur de la Mort*. It was dwarfed by the pirate galleon—and looked kind of shabby next to it, too. Jack looked on with an envious eye as the pirates rushed about efficiently under Captain Smith's command. Ropes were knotted, sails were made ready, anchors were pulled up—and Mr. Reece took Left-Foot Louis and Silverback belowdecks. Someday, Jack told himself. Someday, he would have a ship as fine and grand as this one. With a crew that actually listened to his commands.

Arabella pointedly refused to look at anyone or anything. Her chin stuck out defiantly, and her arms were crossed.

When the captain was finished ordering her men about, Captain Smith turned to her daughter and smiled. Almost nicely.

"You've grown so," she murmured, reaching out a hand to touch Arabella's face.

"Let me alone!" Arabella snapped, slapping her mother's hand away. She turned to face the water, eyes red with angry tears.

Captain Smith looked lost for a moment, for the first time unsure what to do. Then she gritted her teeth and took Jack aside.

"Can I have a word?"

"You can have several," Jack said brightly. "How about: 'good-bye' or 'farewell' or 'here's-your-ship-and-a-nice-pile-of-gold-as-an-unexpected-bonus?'"

Captain Laura Smith frowned. She took Jack by the arm and led him to the railing. "*Captain* Sparrow. Can you please be straight with a long-lost mother? For *just* a moment? How has Arabella been? How long have you known her?"

Jack opened his mouth to say something smart-alecky. But he was stopped by the earnest look on Captain Smith's face. She was dying for news of her daughter. So Jack took a deep breath and told her.

He started with how he first met Arabella—though he left out the bit about Fitzwilliam beating him in a duel. He told her about the city of bones they encountered and the treasure and the tracks they found of Left-Foot Louis (though the treasure was a lot bigger in this version, and the traps even more deadly). He mentioned the sirens and their hypnotic songs and the sea monsters. He alluded briefly to the undead Cortés and the timely intervention of Montezuma. He finished by recounting the crew's mission to recover Tumen's medallion, and their battle against a roomful of zombies.*

"On the whole, except for a tendency to prattle on and be a big know-it-all—" Jack concluded, a little more seriously—"which isn't entirely fair, since she really *does* seem to know it all—Arabella's the best first mate a captain could hope for, and a good friend."

It nearly killed him to be that straight, but Laura's eyes were wide and bright in gratitude.

"Captain Sparrow," she said softly—and not sarcastically, as she had earlier, "may I

*Whew! All this transpired in our first five volumes.

have your permission to speak to your first mate—alone?"

"Well, that is Arabella's decision, mate, I mean *mum*," Jack answered. "But you have my permission if she doesn't mind."

He went across the deck to his first mate who was still staring out over the waves. She stood with her arms folded and her back defiantly toward her mom.

"I'm not talking to her," she said before Jack could say anything.

"Bell," he said, sighing, "I'm not one to agree with Fitzy—ever—but she *is* your mum. My dad never even *tried* to talk to me. Maybe you should hear what she has to say. Then you can do whatever you want, and I'll stand by you. All right, lass?"

"Don't call me 'lass,'" she grumbled.

He clapped her on the back.

"Come on, lads," he said to the rest of his

crew. "There's a . . . um . . . very interesting fishy I want to show you off the prow."

"What fishy?" Tim asked, curiously. Jean kicked his shin.

"Arabella would prefer some private time with her mother," Fitzwilliam explained, dragging the young boy with him across the deck.

Arabella stomped up to her mom and looked her in the eye defiantly.

"Oh, I've missed you so much," Captain Smith said with a hopeful smile.

"I don't buy it, 'Mother,'" Arabella spat. "If ye missed yer own daughter so very much, why did ye find it so important to leave? And never give word of yer being all right?"

Captain Smith sighed, sitting down on a barrel. She gestured for Arabella to join her, but her daughter stayed standing. "It's a long story, love. When I married yer father, running the *Faithful Bride* with him seemed like a nice, cozy little life. But he bought it without knowing the first thing about Tortuga. We thought it was a place for sailors and merchants to relax—not the pirate haven it turned out to be. They were always trashing the place—getting into bloody fights, smashing the furniture, sometimes the walls, often each other's heads. . . ."

Despite herself, Arabella sympathized. It really *did* happen all the time—and as the barmaid, she was often in the thick of it.

"We were always in debt. Honest—*rich*—patrons were scared away by the pirates. Who never paid their tabs, by the way. And any little profits we made went into maintaining the place. You don't remember the leanest years, Arabella. We barely had enough to eat."

Captain Laura's eyes glazed over as she remembered. "I was so scared for you. I wanted to raise you right, with more money and food and things than my own parents gave me growing up." The captain paused. Then she continued, "I had *one* nice dress of my own. From your father's and my wedding. I cut it up to make your baby clothes, Arabella. We couldn't even afford proper cloth that would be soft and fit for a baby."

Arabella turned her head to scratch her nose, so she didn't have to look at her mother's face.

"I *loved* you, Arabella," she said softly. "You were my only joy in that hard life. And we were failing our wee little babe. There weren't a lot of options for an honest family in Tortuga. Well, not a lot of *honest* options." She gave a wry grin and shook her head. Then she sighed and continued. "This is how it happened, love. I had this habit of lis-

tening in on the pirates' conversations—
when you're a barmaid, no one notices you,
you know."

"I know," Arabella answered before she
could stop herself. It was true, and it's what
got Arabella started on this adventure as
part of Jack's crew. Her mother smiled at the
one admission.

"Well, I overheard this one smuggler
telling another how he was havin' a spot of
trouble getting his rum from Rumrunner's
Island to Port Royal. He was always caught,
and his barrels seized, no matter what he
did. And a fierce battle always ensued—he
lost more employees that way, if you take
my drift. He even tried dressing as a lady
once, all in skirts and finery, but he never
could fool the authorities."

Arabella's mother sat up straight, with a
smile, remembering the scene.

"So I say to him, 'Look here, mate—what you need is a *real* lady to smuggle in yer rum for you!' He hired me on the spot. Every new moon—when the sea and night were dark—I boarded his ship, and if we were stopped by the authority, I would act all high-falutin' about them stopping a lady about her business."

Although the image definitely appealed to Arabella, the illegality of it did not. "My mother, the rumrunner," she said, shaking her head.

"I made enough to support us, young lady," Captain Laura said sharply. "At a time when the Faithful Bride was losing money faster than a marine on payday. And your father . . . well, he wasn't working anymore. At anything. He just sat in the back and drank. With drink comes anger. And with anger, violence." The captain shook her head sadly and angrily. "I hoarded my money for months to save for a time when I could take you and leave the Bride and your father forever. Take you someplace nice. Hispaniola, maybe. Or Boston. Or Newfoundland."

"Then a night came, just weeks before I had had enough, when I was double-crossed by me partner, *Left-Foot Louis*."

Arabella's eyes widened in surprise. Then she frowned in suspicion.

"'Partner?' I thought you said you just play-acted a part to get them past the navy and merchant marine. When did you become a 'partner' in this little scheme?"

"Well," her mother said with a faint blush, "it didn't stay so little, you know? After a time, the smuggling became a bit more profitable. . . . I took a larger share . . . and the Bride just became my cover. We branched out into other . . . areas . . . of . . . activity. But let me get back to the telling!" she said impatiently, changing the subject. "Louis took all my money. So one night, when he was in his cups at the Faithful Bride, I took out my pistol and shoved it under his gut!"

"What happened?" Arabella asked breathlessly. Arabella remembered that night, but from a little girl's point of view. All she saw was her mom being dragged out of the tavern. Not the part where her mom attacked a notorious pirate.

"Oh, he was much faster back then. When he was younger," Smith said disgustedly. "Grabbed me by the hair with one hand and grabbed the pistol with the other. He dragged me outside while your father slept upstairs, passed out from the drink."

"I tried to run after you . . ." Arabella said,

remembering. She couldn't have been more than four or five at the time. It was a blurry memory, filled with noise and crying and fear.

". . . and two of Louis's men held you back . . ." her mother continued.

". . . and I never saw you again," Arabella finished sadly.

"You must have been so scared, seeing me taken from you like that . . ." Captain Smith said. "But in the long run, my being taken from the tavern was not such a bad thing. Once outside, Louis stumbled in the rain. I drew my sword. . . ."

"You had a pistol *and* a sword?" Arabella asked incredulously.

"I. Was. *Smuggling*," Captain Laura said deliberately, as if she were spelling it out for her daughter to understand. "So I draw mine, he draws his, and before you know it we're clashing and clanging in the rainy night. 'Course, he's drunk, and I'm mad, so it's hardly surprising when I get the better of him. I grabbed my money back and decided not to take any more chances with useless husbands and double-crossing pirates. I took myself off to a fine boat I had stashed away for just such an emergency. The *Fleur de la Mort*. Aye, she's a very special ship. With a *very* special quality." She patted the railing lovingly.

"So you just left," Arabella said flatly. "You took off in your fancy pirate vessel for the high seas."

"I always intended to return for you, dear," her mother said. "I just . . . didn't want you to know I was a pirate. When I came back, it was going to be as an honest woman with money and a house and a place you could move to, with dresses and toys like you never had. A dowry, if you wanted

to marry. I thought you'd rather believe I was dead than one of the filthy dock rats who drink at the Bride."

Arabella looked at her mother for a long moment, thinking.

Her mother looked hopefully back.

"But you *are* a pirate," Arabella finally said.

"As are you," Captain Smith said with a smile. "You have pirate in your blood."

Arabella's face darkened.

"I am *nothing* like you!" she spat. "I wish you *were* dead, mother!"

Captain Smith frowned at her daughter, setting her jaw. Then she slapped Arabella across the face and stormed off.

CHAPTER FOUR

*J*ack watched Arabella and her mother talking on the other side of the ship. The two
women were so much alike: the way they
stood, the way they frowned, the way their
hair blew back. It was definitely likely that
the two would be making up any moment
now. Well, as likely as Jack sprouting wings
and flying back to the *Barnacle*. He sighed. It
was only a matter of time before real fire-
works between the two women began.

Which meant he had only mere moments

to slip belowdecks to see what was up with Left-Foot Louis and Silverback.

"Here, let's quickly be off below to see what the deal is," Jack said with a conspiratorial grin to his crew.

"How is it you say in English . . . ?" Jean asked jokingly, faking a thicker French accent than he acually had. "Oh yes, *NOT A CHANCE*."

"We already had one tangle with Left-Foot," Tumen agreed. "He is after our blood. And he doesn't play fair—even for a pirate. For all we know he's hiding in the shadows with his dagger, waiting for us."

"Oh, blast the lot of you," Jack muttered, but he couldn't *entirely* blame them. The foul-tempered—not to mention huge and scary—pirate was already in a rage, thanks to Silverback.

He turned with a hopeful grin to Tim

and Fitzwilliam. "Well, boys? Shall we?"

"I, uh, Silverback, uh," Tim stuttered, turning bright red. "He frightens me."

"Fitzy, *please* say at least you'll be joining me in this little jaunt," Jack said, exasperated.

"Normally, I would not hesitate," the aristocrat said. "I should like nothing more than a chance to have a go at a pirate. *But*, I had best stay here to receive Arabella, after she and her mother finish conversing. This has been an exhausting day for her, and no doubt she will need emotional support."

Jack narrowed his eyes at Fitzwilliam. "All right, you lily-livered lot! You all stay up here with your *histories* and your *blood feuds* and your *ladies*. I, Captain Jack Sparrow, am going below. Alone. No—don't bother volunteering now, it's too late," he added, holding up his hand and walking away. "Too late."

Jack tried to be inconspicuous. He

pretended to be inspecting the ship: rapping on barrels, examining a sail, running a finger along a rail and seeing if he could find a trace of dust. When he was sure no one was looking, he jumped down the hatch.

"I wonder if Captain Laura's cabin is all girly," Jack mused to himself, sneaking down the corridor. He pressed his back up against the bulkhead and wedged himself into the shadows. "Lace on her bunk . . . little, I don't know, frilly things. Flowers decorating the place . . ."

Two familiar-looking pirate shapes lumbered down the hall. Jack immediately shut his trap and looked for a place to blend into his surroundings. Unfortunately, there was nothing nearby except for a couple of smelly, slimy-looking barrels.

But the pirates were coming closer, and there was nowhere else to go.

Jack sighed, held his nose, and jumped into the closest barrel. He landed with a wet *thud* on a pile of stinky, wet rubbery things. He held his breath as best he could. In the darkness he felt around the wood until he found a wooden plug filling the bunghole. He pressed it hard with his thumb. It popped out—with more noise than he intended. Jack flinched. No one seemed to have heard it, though. When he pressed his eye to the now-open hole he had a perfect view.

Jack could see Silverback and Louis. He waited expectantly for the explosions to begin.

Except there weren't any.

"Care to have my grog ration tonight?" Left-Foot offered politely.

"Oh, thank you, that would be lovely," Silverback responded, equally politely. "Is your liver acting up again?"

"Oh, it's in a terrible state," Left-Foot Louis bemoaned.

What was going on?

Something on Silverback glittered in the low light—and it wasn't his tooth or his leg this time. It was around his neck—a silver charm at the end of a leather cord. It looked a lot like a gem. In fact, it looked *quite* a lot like the piece of bronze that was set in the Sun-and-Stars medallion. Could it be the second gem? The number of coincidences connected to that blasted amulet was increasing very quickly. Jack grinned. And here he was, in the middle of it all . . .

. . . not that he *wanted* its power. He was done with curses and magic. Like he said. But *mysteries* . . . Well, that was something else. Wouldn't it be nice to know what the medallion was truly capable of?

"Laura's still completely fooled, isn't she?

We pulled the wool over her eyes," Left-Foot said with a rotten, toothy grin.

"For now, yes," Silverback said, nodding. "She still thinks we hate each other. That we're at each other's throats. We must be careful to maintain this ruse. I think the time is drawing nigh to execute our plan."

"Aye," Louis said with a growl. "Once we get our mates to take over the ship, I can return to the *Cutlass*. Go back to being a proper captain again."

"And I can take over the *Fleur*," Silverback said with a gleam in his eye. "I don't think it will take much to incite the crew. Captain Laura runs a little too tight a ship— for pirates, anyway."

They were planning a mutiny, Jack realized with horror. The foulest crime on the high seas. Instant hanging offense, no matter what your alignment—navy, merchant, *or* pirate. These two were the worst of the worst.

"It's a little more complicated now with her daughter and her weird little friends," Silverback pointed out.

Weird? Fine. But *Little*? Jack took offense at that.

"Now she's got allies," Louis agreed. "It could be a problem."

Silverback laughed. "I said *complicated*, not a problem. They're just children, Louis."

"Oh, aye, but . . ." Louis looked around, then leaned forward to whisper into the other pirate's ear. It was obvious that Silverback didn't appreciate the gesture, or Louis's breath. "Don't be fooled. I know they *look* just like wee barnes . . . but they're a force to contend with. Trust me on this one. Especially the *cat*."

"Oh, don't be ridiculous, Louis," Silverback said, waving his hand in dismissal. "A cat, indeed. We'll get rid of them and then Mr. Reece. It will be quick. We'll have no more obstacles to our mission."

Now it was Jack's turn to sneer. It wouldn't be easy *or* quick. Nor would they succeed. Louis was right. The crew of the *Barnacle* really was a force to be reckoned with. And once Arabella and Captain Smith made up, they would join forces and overcome this mutiny.

Assuming Arabella and her mom actually made up.

Now what were the two pirates doing? Jack wondered. While Jack was being all smug, they had stopped talking . . .

Then he saw Louis come back into view . . . and head straight for the barrel.

Jack gulped, and held his breath. It was like Louis somehow knew exactly where Jack was. He leaned over and reached in!

Jack panicked, pressing himself up against

the slimy wood. He frantically grabbed one of the slippery, rubbery things that he was sitting on and shoved it into Louis hand.

Louis pulled his hand out. Apparently, it was what he was reaching for after all. He had no idea Jack was in there, too.

"So the mutiny will take place tonight at dusk," Silverback said.

"Aye," Louis nodded and offered him the slimy thing. It was a fish! Head and all. Mostly raw and only half-pickled. Silverback shook his head. Louis shrugged and shoved it into his mouth, head first. With a contented growl he ripped off a chunk. Then he chewed with satisfied, smacking noises.

Jack shuddered. He couldn't imagine eating a fish like that . . . at least, not without some paprika sprinkled on top.

CHAPTER FIVE

$\mathcal{B}$ack on deck, Arabella was rubbing her face where her mother had slapped her. Okay, she probably deserved that a little bit. And she didn't *really* wish her mother were dead. But it really hurt that she had never even sent word . . . all those years. . . . Just knowing that her mother was actually alive would have made things so much more bearable.

Captain Laura Smith was looking out over the sea, still fuming. Then she sighed deeply and went back to her daughter.

"I . . ." Arabella began, unsure of what was going to come out. Forgiveness? Anger? "I thought you were *dead*. Couldn't you have gotten me some word . . . somehow. . . ."

Whatever her mother was about to say next was lost forever when First Mate Reece approached and interrupted them.

"Beg pardon, Captain. But I've just finished looking at the charts. If these winds keep up, we should be in Port Royal in a little less than a day," he said.

"Excellent, Mr. Reece. And the East India Trading Company ship we're scheduled to intercept?"

Mr. Reece grinned. "Right on target, Captain. According to our sources."

All of Arabella's confusion about her mother vanished. "Oh, right. I forgot. Not only did you run away from your only daughter for life on the high seas, but you're also a *pirate*," she said disgustedly.

"You should have all the facts before going about accusing people," her mother said sharply. "The captain of the ship we're going to seize already knows about our little heist. In fact, he helped plan it. We're going to split the profits."

"And this is better, how?" Arabella snarled. "People could still get killed in the fight! And it's *still stealing!*"

Her mother rolled her eyes and patted her daughter on the head. As if to say: you're too young to understand. Arabella stomped away, toward a concerned-looking Fitzwilliam.

Meanwhile, Jack had waited until the coast was clear to come out of his stinky barrel. He popped his head out of the hatch to see if anyone was looking, then sprang up onto the deck. He practically fell over himself running toward Arabella.

"There, there, do not be too upset," Fitzwilliam was saying to her, arms open for a comforting hug. "Your mother just . . ."

"Yes yes, no time for that now," Jack said, grabbing Arabella and steering her away. Fitzwilliam's face fell.

Jack put an arm around Arabella's shoulder, pretending to comfort her.

"You *stink*, Jack," Arabella said, holding her nose and pushing Jack away.

Curious, he took a whiff of himself. Unfortunately, he had to agree. He was sopping in half-pickled fish juices. "Sorry about that. But look, we've got a problem, Bell-me-lass."

"Get away from me, Jack" she said, angry to the point of tears. "I'm in no mood for yer games!"

Jack sighed and tightened his grip so she couldn't get away. "No, a *real* problem, my faithful first mate. I did a little legwork on the couple-of-the-year there, Silverback and Left-Foot Louis. Turns out they're actually in cahoots; demonical, piratical cahoots! They've planned a mutiny for tonight, and it sounds like they have most of the ship on their side."

Arabella's eyes widened at the word *mutiny*. Usually when pirates were sick of a captain, they just demoted him (or her) and picked a new one. It was one of the only civilized, bloodless things they did.

Then she shrugged.

"So what. Good riddance. My mother's a pirate—she chose a life of villainy and bloodshed. Serves her right."

Jack closed his eyes in exasperation. So rarely did any of his crew ever stop to see the big picture.

"All right, Bell. First thing. You have *got* to let this thing with your mother go. Drop it. Just for a moment. Second thing. It's not your dear mum I'm worried about, lass. Louis and Silverback have said they are going to come after *us*—you and me and everyone on the *Barnacle*—first, because they have some wacky notion that because you're Captain Laura's daughter you would help her out."

Arabella frowned, trying to figure out what Jack was driving at.

"We. Have. To. Get. Off. This. Ship." Jack spelled it out for her impatiently. "Savvy?"

Arabella looked a little uncertain. "But how will we do that?"

Jack squinted at the horizon. The sun lay right above it, beginning to mellow in the late afternoon. "We only have a little while before dusk—everyone is going to be ramping up for this mutiny thing. Tell the others—*quietly*—to start heading toward the *Barnacle*. Once the commotion starts, no one will notice us slipping over the side. It should be easy in the confusion, as long as we don't run afoul of Silverback and Louis. I'll see if I can loosen the ropes now, while no one's looking."

Arabella nodded mutely. She went over to Fitzwilliam first, who was pretending to be interested in a particular knot in the rigging. He had been trying to listen in on her and Jack, but the wind wasn't right.

"Be prepared to leave," she said, also pretending to look at the knot. "There's going to be a mutiny. Start heading—casual, like— to the *Barnacle*. If me mother—if *Captain Smith* spots you, just pretend you're doing something else. No one else will care."

"Mutiny?" Fitzwilliam mouthed. Then he

sneered. "I would expect no better of these
. . . pirates," he hissed.

Arabella just ignored him, moving on
toward Jean and Tumen. She had no desire
to get into a discussion with the aristocrat
about how this was unusual behavior for
pirates. How their leadership was actually
quite democratic: the captain was elected,
and the profits were shared equally. A much
better system than any of the private merchant ships, really . . . if you didn't mind the
looting and pillaging. . . . And the powers
that be would never let a woman be in
charge of a 'proper' ship. . . .

Arabella shook her head. Was she feeling sympathy for her mother's chosen pro-
fession? She wouldn't allow it. She bit her
lip and sneaked a glance at her mother.
Captain Laura was giving some order, in
high spirits, the wind blowing her hair back,

a fierce smile on her face. The pirate who she spoke to nodded and hurried away—at least he *looked* like he was fully devoted to her.

All Arabella really wanted with the Sword of Cortés, and the treasure, and these adventures, was freedom. Freedom to be able to be her own woman—and here was her mum, already doing just that.

And now her treacherous crew was going to take it all away. And probably *kill* her.

"*M'mselle*," Jean said as Arabella came up to him. "You seem a little . . . out of sorts." He and Tumen were sitting on barrels, looking like they were enjoying themselves despite their situation. A pile of several banana peels lay on the deck, and Tumen's mouth was still full.

"The crew is planning a mutiny," she said, still looking at her mother. "While everyone is distracted with that, we're to head to the *Barnacle* and escape."

"But your mother," Jean said with concern, "will she be all right?"

"I . . . don't know," Arabella said. As much as she had wished her ill—or thought she did—it really was different from seeing her forced to walk the plank by her own crew.

Jack watched Arabella as he sneaked over to where his ship was tied to the *Fleur*. She was obviously worried about her mum, no matter how much she pretended she wasn't. He sighed. They would probably wind up having to figure out some way to rescue *her*, too.

Louis and Silverback climbed out of the hatch, 'fighting' as usual.

"Yer a yellow-bellied, scrawny whelp of a man!" Louis bellowed with enthusiasm.

Mr. Reece saw the two and frowned. He

marched up to them, his bright blue eyes blazing. "May I remind you the Captain has ordered that you remain below deck for a time?"

Silverback turned to the first mate and grinned—a nasty, leering grin. His tooth flashed blue, and the first mate of the *Fleur de la Mort* disappeared.

Jack was idly wondering where he had disappeared to, when Silverback turned to *him*. Like he knew he was watching all along. His tooth and leg were still flashing blue.

"And you're next," Silverback said threateningly, smiling at Jack.

CHAPTER SIX

*J*ack thought fast.

Silverback's crystal leg and tooth had flashed red when he made the sword fly from Left-Foot's right hand. It was *yellow* when he was somehow figuring out all the details of Jack and his friends' lives.

And it was *blue*—just as it was now—when they were magicked off the *Barnacle* and onto the *Fleur*.

Silverback was going to disappear him away somewhere!

On the upside, it would probably be off the ship. On the downside, it could be anywhere—including Davy Jones's Locker. Jack figured it would be best if he played it safe.

"You probably don't want to do that, mate," Jack said casually as the blue light strobed faster and faster.

His tone caught Silverback's attention. The pirate frowned, and the blue light slowed. Jack pulled the Sun-and-Stars medallion out. The one the crew should have been on their way to returning to Tumen's people. The one that had them all off on this ridiculous, seemingly never-ending adventure. Jack dangled it enticingly from its cord.

"Judging by that pretty little charm you have hanging 'round your neck, it looks like you might be in need of this," Jack said, pointing at the silver 'bullet' Silverback wore—the one that matched the bronze gem already in the medallion.

The pirate's face grew red with fury. *"My medallion!"* he cried.

"Well, now, that's sort of a complicated issue, isn't it?" Jack said calmly, swinging the medallion as carelessly as if it were a yo-yo. "The people of my friend's village claim it's theirs—they've been holding it for some *other* people for umpty-ump years. And then there's Madame Minuit, a fearsome— and often attractive—magicks queen, who would also like to think it's *her* medallion. And now you're saying it's *your* medallion. But possession is nine-tenths of the law, as they say. And currently *I'm* possessing it."

Silverback raked out his hand, trying to snatch the medallion away. With barely a twitch, Jack slid back a foot.

"You may as well just hand it over,"

Silverback said with a sneer. "My powers are greater than you could possibly imagine."

"Hmm," Jack said, unconcerned. He continued to play with the medallion, and wondered what the pirate would look like turned to bronze. Might make a nice hat rack. He slid back another foot.

"You have no idea what you're holding," Silverback pointed out, stepping forward again. "A mere child like you. You could never use the medallion to its full potential."

"I'm a quick learner," Jack disagreed, with a grin.

"*GIVE ME BACK MY MEDALLION!*" Silverback screamed, completely losing his temper. He lunged. Jack leaped back.

Silverback gritted his teeth. The crystal tooth and his leg began to glow red.

Arabella, still feeling guilty about abandoning her mother and wondering what to do, looked up and saw what was going on with Jack and the pirate. In that moment, her thoughts cleared and she knew exactly what course of action to take.

"You'll have to get through me first!" she cried, leaping in between Silverback and Jack. She drew her sword and flourished it in the pirate's face.

"Uh, Bell," Jack said in a stage whisper, "Not that I don't appreciate your enthusiasm, but methinks I can handle my own battles here. . . ."

"Mother!" Arabella called out. Captain Laura Smith looked up from where she was going over a chart with her navigator. "These men plan to mutiny aboard yer ship!" Arabella continued.

"Um, Bell, wait—remember?" Jack asked out the side of his mouth. "The plan? *They* mutiny? *We* escape?"

Arabella's mother quickly surveyed the situation. All of her crew had begun to draw their knives and swords. Even the navigator she was just talking to had his rapier out and a rotten-toothed grin on his face.

"Vermin! Traitorous thugs!" Captain Laura spat. She drew her cutlass. "*En garde!*"

Jack sighed. Jean and Tumen and Tim and Fitzwilliam were paused, midsneak, on their way back to the *Barnacle*. They looked at their captain questioningly.

"All right, lads, come on," Jack said, waving at them. "It's pirates this time, not a creepy, beautiful snake lady.* Swords out!"

---

*Jack is referring to Madame Minuit, who the crew faced in our last volume, *The Age of Bronze*.

CHAPTER SEVEN

*F*or a moment, all was still aboard the *Fleur de la Mort*. She quietly bobbed on a calm sea, the *Barnacle* tied closely to her side. White puffy clouds floated overhead.

Then with an animal-like snarl, Left-Foot Louis charged Captain Laura Smith. The entire deck broke out in fighting.

Jack shoved the medallion back into his pocket and drew his bronzed cutlass on Silverback. "It's all right, lass, leave this one to me," he told Arabella.

Arabella nodded, and with a loud cry, rushed over to the knot of pirates advancing on her mother.

Silverback grinned at Jack and his tooth started to flash red—

—then Jack struck Silverback's crystal leg full-on with the blade of his sword. It rang like a bell. The vibrations traveled up his leg and through Silverback's body.

Silverback shook himself free and prepared to concentrate again, his tooth beginning to glow—

—and Jack struck his leg again. Higher up, to see if it made a different sound.

It did. Jack cleared his throat and hummed, trying to match the key.

"*Blow high and blow low, and so sailed we . . .*" he sang.

"Cut that out!" Silverback demanded.

"Then fight like a man, not like a sorcerer,"

Jack growled, attacking him in earnest.

"Fine, I can beat you any way you want, you whelp!" Silverback promised, drawing his sword. The two dove at each other madly.

Farther up the deck, the crew of the *Barnacle* joined the fray.

"I do not understand, who we are fighting." Fitzwilliam said, confused. "The pirates, or just the mutinous pirates? Or the people in charge of the mutinous pirates?"

"Anyone who raises a sword," Tim Hawk suggested helpfully, pulling out his own little knife and charging.

"It looks like there's about three of them for every one of us," Tumen observed, standing back-to-back with Jean as they both fended off vicious pirates.

"Those are odds just the way I like them!" Jean said with a wolfish grin. "As Madame Captain said—*en garde*!"

A pair of pirates, one with a sword and one with something that looked suspiciously like a scythe, advanced on Jean. With a grin the boy leapt and spun, holding his rapier out as far as it would go. The tip sliced through the pirates' shirts and grazed their stomachs. They sucked in their guts to avoid being cut—and Jean dropped to the deck and rolled. He knocked into the legs of the one closest to him. The pirate toppled, falling onto his friend.

Tumen had his long obsidian knife out. Its shiny black blade flashed wickedly in the sunlight. A frustrated pirate with a black eye patch and matching bandana kept lunging at him with a rusty old cutlass. But Tumen was too fast for him. *And* too short. He was able to duck and weave, avoiding every strike.

"Stay still, mouse!" the pirate roared.

"All right," Tumen agreed. He froze, then quickly brought his dagger up at an unexpected angle. With barely a whisper of ripped cloth, it cut his opponent's hand. Howling and grabbing his bleeding arm, the pirate fell to the deck. His cutlass flew through the air. Tumen leapt nimbly on top of him, catching the sword as it fell.

"A mouse that *roars*," Tumen said.

Fitzwilliam was using his famous fancy footwork to fight two pirates at once. He advanced, pushing them backward to the prow. His shiny sword glittered and clanged. He parried their every blow with ease.

"Yes! Retreat, you blackguards!" Fitzwilliam called out enthusiastically.

It wasn't quite the glorious duel against villains that the nobleman's son had always imagined. Rather than rallying against him for a good fight, the cowards kept backing up, away from his blows.

And when they finally ran out of deck,

they went over the ship's rail, where they tumbled into the sea.

Meanwhile, Tim Hawk ducked around a barrel, baiting a giant pirate into chasing him. He popped his head out the left side and made a face. The pirate slashed at him, but Tim quickly withdrew and then popped his head out the *right* side. The pirate missed again. Tim kept moving and the pirate kept slashing, always missing the boy by inches.

Finally, the pirate brought his sword down too hard. It stuck in the barrel's wood. Tim ducked in between the pirate's legs while he was busy trying to free his blade—and pulled the pirate's pants down around his ankles. The giant pirate howled with frustration, unable to get his sword out and pull his pants up at the same time.

Arabella was distracted fighting two pirates of her own. Being a barmaid in a dangerous tavern had taught her quite a few tactics over the years. But she couldn't help nervously keeping an eye on her mother and Left-Foot Louis as they sparred a few feet away from her. It was like reliving that horrible night in the Faithful Bride so many years before. Any moment she expected Louis to win, grabbing her mother and hauling her away . . . again. . . .

"I've been waiting *months* for this," Left-Foot said with an evil grin. He wasn't as quick as he had been years ago, but he was definitely stronger. It took all of Captain Laura's energy and skill to avoid his sword each time he tried to swing it down on her.

"I should have killed you when I had the chance," she growled. "A *mutinous* pirate. You're a real scoundrel, Left-Foot."

"I like to think so, Madam Captain," Louis replied.

Fitzwilliam slid past them back down the deck, fighting off *three* pirates this time. And the pirates were winning. There was a red gash across Fitzwilliam's forehead, and his blue jacket and red vest were torn.

"How you doin' there, mate?" Jack called out, parrying a blow from Silverback, who was a much better swordsman than Jack had guessed.

"Because you asked, I could use another sword at my side," Fitzwilliam admitted.

"Here, begging your pardon a moment," Jack said politely to Silverback. Then he spun and with the back of his pommel knocked another pirate in the head. As he toppled to the ground, his cutlass flew up. Jack caught it and tossed it to Fitzwilliam.

"How's that?" Jack asked, turning back to continue his fight with Silverback.

"Not exactly what I meant, but it will do,"

Fitzwilliam said with a grin. He caught the sword in his left hand and renewed the attack on his assailants with *both* blades. And he was equally good with each.

"The gig's up," Jack told Silverback in between blows.

"Hardly," Silverback replied. But he looked nervous.

The tide of fighting on the boat was definitely turning. Fitzwilliam, Jean, Tumen, and Tim Hawk made a team effort to herd the almost-defeated pirates to the center of the deck, conveniently near the hatch. The casualties were piling up, and the mutineers were quickly becoming dismayed.

Laura and Left-Foot were still dueling. The captain's sword was broken in half, but she still managed to parry with the pommel. Louis was advancing on her with a crazed look in his eyes.

Silverback turned his attention to them. "Left-Foot, forget the captain. We should make our escape. . . ."

"Not with this you don't!" Jack yelled.

He seized the moment—Silverback was distracted. With a delicate move, Jack lashed out the very tip of his sword to the pirate's neck. He hooked the cord with the silver bullet on the end and yanked it over Silverback's head. The necklace flew through the air, landing with a comforting *thwack* in Jack's hand.

Silverback clutched his throat with his hands, dropping his sword. "The gem!" he screamed.

Jack leveled his cutlass at Silverback's chest, pushing him up against a mast. "The gem's not all you have to worry about there, mate."

Left-Foot Louis barely noticed his fellow

mutineer's defeat, so intent was he on over-
throwing Arabella's mother. With a growl,
he backed her up against the other side of
the mast. Captain Smith gasped. Louis
raised his sword above his head and brought
it down with both his meaty hands—

—and Captain Smith drew a knife out.
She crossed it over what was left of her own
broken sword and caught Louis's blade
between them.

With a bloodcurdling cry she brought the
blades apart, spinning the sword out of
Louis's hands and over the side of the boat.
Then she kicked him in the ribs. When he
went down, she raised her knife, ready to cut
his throat.

"NO!" Arabella and Silverback cried out
at the same time.

And then Left-Foot and Silverback disappeared . . .

CHAPTER EIGHT

Captain Smith threw her knife down on the deck in frustration.

"Where did they go?" Fitzwilliam asked curiously.

"Look." Tumen pointed. Off the port side of the ship, a little rowboat was speedily pulling away into the sea—with no one rowing it. Left-Foot Louis sat in the back. Silverback stood in the front, his leg glowing a dark, sickly red. It was eerie the way they steadily glided over the sea, without the familiar push-pull of oars, using only the power of Silverback's crystals.

"AFTER THEM!" Captain Laura ordered.

Everyone just looked at her.

"Who, exactly, are you talking to, Madam Captain?" Jack asked with mock politeness. Jean and Tim were rounding up the last few pirates and locking them in the—now incredibly cramped—brig. The unconscious were unceremoniously pushed through the hatch.

There was hardly anyone left on the deck except for Laura and the crew of the *Barnacle*—in the end, almost her entire ship had mutinied.

"All right, then, quarter shares for you all!" Laura promised. "Right after we hit the East India Trading Company. But for now, man the sails and the wheel, and *get after those scallywags!*"

"Begging your pardon again, Madam Captain," Jack said patiently, "but what for?"

"They fomented mutiny! They attacked their captain! They ran off before I could make them walk the plank!" Laura yelled.

Arabella rolled her eyes. "A bit dramatic there, mother?"

Jack ticked points off on his fingers. "We still have the medallion—no, wait, don't interrupt," he added quickly, holding a hand up before Captain Smith could speak. "Arabella will explain it all to you later, no doubt. Medallion: we still have it. We also now have Silverback's gem. *You* still have this fabulous boat. And I'm sure you'll be able to get yourself a newer, better crew just like that," Jack said, snapping his fingers.

"Surely she could not get a much worse one," Fitzwilliam muttered.

"The point is, we all have everything we need. Right here." Jack waved his hand. "A boat, a magic medallion, and a star to steer us all by. Or something. Look, just let it go, all right, then, Arabella's mum?"

Laura bit her lip again, just like Arabella. One last time, she glared furiously at the boat disappearing toward the horizon.

"Your words make a certain amount of sense," she admitted grudgingly.

"That must be the very first time someone has told you that," Fitzwilliam teased Jack.

"Stay back!" Jean suddenly yelled. Everyone turned to look. He had a very wet and tired looking Mr. Reece at sword point. His red bandana had flopped down over one blue eye, and a fish was stuck in his belt.

"It's all right," Jack said, waving his arm to hold back his friends. "He's the only one still loyal to the captain on this blasted boat."

Jean lowered his sword but looked untrusting.

"Mr. Reece!" Captain Smith cried with a

grin. She winked at the handsome first mate. "I *knew* you were a good man!"

"He's still a pirate," Arabella said snootily.

"Where were you during all the fighting?" Fitzwilliam demanded.

"More important, why in the Seven Seas did you bother coming back?" Jack muttered. "With all this drama going on . . ." He waved his hands.

"Silverback used his devilish powers and magicked me away. Before the mutiny got underway, I suppose," Mr. Reece said tiredly, using a finger to get water out of his ear. "But his range isn't very far. I think he meant to drown me—I suddenly found myself several feet underwater. I kicked to the surface and clung to the side of the ship. I've been trying to get myself back up the entire time. Sorry I missed the excitement." He gave Captain Smith a nod that was almost a bow. "I would have defended you with my life, you know that."

Laura beamed.

"You have a fish in your belt," Arabella pointed out sourly.

Mr. Reece sighed, his dignity completely gone. He pulled the flopping fish out and tossed it into a nearby barrel.

"Now that we've had all of these charming reunions," Jack said, pressing his hands together, "daughter and mother, first mate and captain, silver gem and medallion . . . might I ask what you plan to do, Captain Laura, with the mutinous crew of yours we've locked belowdecks?"

"Throw them all overboard," Arabella's mother said. "Drown the lot of them."

"Mother!" Arabella protested.

"Sounds reasonable to me," Mr. Reece said thoughtfully.

"Pardon my interfering, but do they not need to be tried, or something of that sort?" Fitzwilliam asked.

"Mutinous pirates? They'd be hung immediately," Tumen pointed out.

"We could leave them on a deserted island," Jean suggested.

Captain Smith looked thoughtful. "Are there any in the area? Preferably without drinking water?"

"So they'll die of *thirst*? Mother, that's terrible!" Arabella said with horror.

"Actually, we were just recently stranded on a deserted island,"* Tumen said helpfully.

"Only it's not deserted anymore. And there's lots of water there, with all that snow," Jean reminded him.

"Forget it, then," Captain Smith said. "Drown them, like I originally said."

*Back in Volume 4: *The Sword of Cortés*

"Um, *excuse* me, and pardon me for interrupting," Jack said politely. "But while we're all debating the various merits of drowning, hanging, or dehydrating your crew, may I point out the *ship*—the big one over there, with all the flags and things—that is rapidly heading our way?"

Everyone turned to look.

Approaching from the opposite direction in which Silverback and Louis had gone—a giant, trim-looking vessel was coming speedily at them. A giant, trim-looking vessel with a lot of cannons. And British flags fluttering off its masts.

"It's a navy ship," Fitzwilliam immediately realized.

"That's it then. It will be hanging for *all* of us," Jack said darkly.

CHAPTER NINE

$\mathcal{T}$he navy ship increased its speed. Jack took Fitzwilliam's spyglass—the aristocrat didn't protest this time. If there was any stray doubt about being noticed by the other vessel, it was erased by what Jack saw. The military scurrying around on deck, the cannons being readied, the captain—in a magnificent hat— pointing at the *Fleur* and barking orders.

"Sort of makes you wonder what the point of a Jolly Roger is," Jack observed, looking up at the flag above. Captain Laura's flag was tailored to her: a skull with cross *roses*, where cross*bones* would normally be. It stood out. "Maybe pirates would be more successful if they went undercover? Didn't advertise the fact, et cetera?" Jack said.

"Quickly! Unfurl the sails!" Captain Smith ordered everyone.

They just stood there, looking at her.

"Please," she added after a moment.

Arabella, Tim, Jean, and Tumen looked at Jack. Shockingly, even Fitzwilliam did. Jack gave them a brief nod. The four boys hurried off to carry out Laura's orders.

"I love a good last desperate attempt as much as the next adventurer," Jack said, turning to Arabella's mother. "But may I take the sad responsibility of pointing out that there is *no* chance of us escaping them? With the *Barnacle* tied to the *Fleur*'s side, she's as maneuverable as a sea cow with pleurisy. By the time we even catch the wind, well, *they'll* have caught up to *us*. Savvy?"

Captain Laura just gave him a grin. "Watch and learn, laddie!"

Jean and Tumen let loose a line and the sails came billowing down. They were beautiful, a blue that blended perfectly with the Caribbean sky. A whispery, spiderweb-soft sheen glowed off them. The cloth fluttered under the slightest breeze.

Slowly, laboriously, with the *Barnacle* in tow, the *Fleur de la Mort* began to move. The navy ship was so close now that Jack could read the name (the *Pride of London*) and see the black shine on its cannons. The crew of the *Barnacle* gritted their teeth and waited tensely . . . but Captain Laura and Mr. Reece didn't seem bothered at all.

"You have right beautiful sails," Jack said. "But I still don't see . . ."

Suddenly the naval ship slowed down. Jack raised an eyebrow at Laura, but she just gave him a mysterious smile. He looked through the spyglass again. There seemed to be some sort of confusion on deck. The *Pride* turned slightly to the east. Slowly. The captain and his first mate were shouting at each other. Then the naval ship straightened and turned west a little. It continued like that, weaving across the sea like a drunken sailor searching for his heading.

Finally it passed the *Fleur*. It came close enough so that if its oars had been out, the tips would have been broken off. The crew on the *Pride* seemed to be looking everywhere over the water—everywhere except directly at the *Fleur*, that is. It was spooky.

"What in blazes is going on here?" Jack demanded.

"That's the beauty of the *Fleur de la Mort*,"

Captain Laura said proudly. "Her sails were woven in the islands of Samoa by some mystic fishermen who live there. We are invisible to all but those aboard this ship."

"Well," Jack said with genuine admiration. Imagine having a ship like that! He could go anywhere. . . . What a grand idea . . .

"Aye, we're free to go," Laura said, giving an ironic wave to the naval boat. It continued confusedly sailing this way and that into the distance, still looking for the pirate ship that had disappeared before the crew's eyes. Soon that story would join the many other great sea myths of the Caribbean.

"Heading?" Tumen asked politely, taking out his astrolabe as Jean took the wheel.

"New Orleans," Captain Smith said decisively. "It is the nearest port, and despite my earlier trepidation, I am certain we will find there the mutinous slime who tried to

commandeer my ship. Bringing them to justice is far more important than intercepting
that trading company ship. I'll explain
myself to my partner later."

"Actually, *mother*," Arabella said with her
nose in the air and hands on her hips, "*We*—
my friends and I—and notice the term
friends, there—have to go in the *opposite*
direction. To the Yucatán, to return a treasure to our *friend* Tumen's village. Like we
promised. See, it's all about loyalty and
promises . . . but ye wouldn't know much
about that, would ye, Mother?"

"You will *not* speak to me that way—
either as a captain or as your mother!" Laura
said with icy fury.

"You're not my captain. *Jack* is. And I
notice ye didn't answer me question,"
Arabella said, sticking out her lower lip.
"The part about loyalty and promises . . . ?"

"You insolent girl! I am extremely loyal to my friends and allies!" Captain Smith said, hands clenching and unclenching as if she wanted to smack someone again.

"But not daughters, it seems," Arabella said scornfully.

"Um," Jack said, getting a little uncomfortable. He traded a look with Fitzwilliam, who was also shifting nervously.

"I *told* you my story! I guess I shouldn't expect *little girls* to understand the difficult choices adults have to make," Captain Smith said with a sniff.

"*Difficult choices*? You abandoned your child because you didn't like the life you had!" Arabella's voice began to get shrieky.

"Uh," Jack said again. Mr. Reece was carefully studying the deck. Tumen and Jean were fidgeting.

"*Some* of us didn't have a . . . a . . . 'Jack' to

96

save us from it all!" Captain Laura shouted back, leaning forward into her daughter's face.

"*I AM NOT A DAMSEL IN DISTRESS!!! HE DIDN'T SAVE ME!*" Arabella screamed.

That was it. Jack raised his eyebrows and moved his head in the direction of the hatch. Relieved beyond words, Tim, Fitzwilliam, Jean, and Tumen eagerly rushed belowdecks to escape the mother-and-daughter feud. Mr. Reece looked like he sorely wished he could go with them, but he was a loyal first mate. Jack came quickly after. Neither Arabella nor Captain Laura Smith noticed.

The five boys gathered in the captain's office, which had a nice large table they could all sit around. But even though there were several layers of wood and tar and planking between them and the deck, the two women could still be heard screaming at each other up above.

". . . Useless bar brat!"

". . . *SEA COW!*"

Jack winced. "Fitzy, light us a lantern, would you?"

The aristocrat did as he was told. He set it in the middle of the thick wooden table. Jack carefully laid the medallion out in front of him. It glinted, reflecting the lantern's flames. Then he took out the silver gem he had swiped from Silverback and laid it next to the medallion.

"Where on earth did you get *that*?" Fitzwilliam asked in surprise. None of them had seen the fight with Silverback, or seen Jack take the gem from him.

"A pirate gave it to me," Jack said whimsically. "Looks like a good fit, doesn't it?" He moved it so it was near an open setting in the medallion, next to the bronze one.

"That gem—it's mine!" Tim cried out.

Everyone stared at him. The crew was taken aback. They didn't know him very well—they had only just picked him up in New Orleans, and he had previously been working with the villainous Madame Minuit.* Had they trusted him too quickly?

Tim shrank back a bit. "I mean, my family's," he explained more calmly. But he never took his eyes off the silver gem.

"This whole medallion thing is getting stranger and stranger," Jack said slowly. "Maybe you'd better explain yourself, lad. Start from the beginning."

Tim cleared his throat, a little reluctant to tell his sad story. "It's been in my family for generations. My great-great grandfather, Jebediah Hawk, acquired it on one of his expeditions to the New World—the Hawks

*This all took place in Vol. 5, *The Age of Bronze*

still lived in England back then. My da' never thought it was anything special, just a souvenir from a trip. A charm. It's just silver, after all. But it was one of the few things our family had, you know?" His face darkened, remembering. "Silverback came looking for it two years ago. . . . It was a horrible night . . . his leg and terrible grin all glowing red like fire . . . everything in the house flying around . . . I'd never seen anything like it. Before that time, nothing out of the ordinary had happened to me—or anyone I knew for that matter. Wizards and magic and supernatural things were things you read about, not things you *lived*. I didn't know there really were wizards! Or pirates. Or pirate wizards. I thought they was just stories my da' told me."

He took a deep breath. "Silverback destroyed everything, looking for the gem. I

remember him screaming like a madman. '*Where is it? Where's the silver bullet?*' Then his leg and face glowed this horrible yellow. And he turned, looking right at me. My father grabbed me and pushed me out the back door and made me run away. When I looked back all I saw were flames—and Silverback still grinning. I don't know what happened to my mom and da'."

His eyes were very bright with memory in the lantern light.

"There now, lad," Fitzwilliam said a little awkwardly.

"Go on," Jack prodded the boy.

"I stowed away on the first fishing vessel I could find that was headed to Barbados," Tim continued after collecting himself. "My uncle lives there. I thought I could live with him, and together we could find my family. Maybe they were still alive. Maybe they were already on their way to see him. But then we made a port of call at the mouth of the Pantano River. I left the boat for a little while—just enough time to find or steal some food. A stranger approached me. He was dressed all in rags and looked crazy, with all these dead snakes hanging around his neck. . . ."

Jack's eyebrows raised. He immediately recognized the description of the old man in rags. It was the same disguise Madame Minuit used when the crew confronted her in New Orleans.*

"Madame Minuit!" Jack said.

The boy nodded grimly.

"She grabbed my arm and told my own story back to me. The gem, my home going up in flames, the fact that I was looking for my parents . . . and she told me she would help me, if I did as she said."

* In Vol. 5, The Age of Bronze

"What did you do?" Fitzwilliam asked.

The boy gave him a look. "A crazy 'man' with dead snakes hanging around his neck who can read your mind asks you to 'do some things for him'? What do ya *think* I did? I told him I would seriously think about it. And I seriously thought about turning around and running the other way."

"I'm with you there, lad," Jack said, getting the point.

"I waited too long to say anything, and then one of his—her—snakes came alive and bit me. As you know, a snake bite from Madame will possess you. So, I was hypnotized. From that moment on, I was under her spell," Tim finished, shrugging helplessly. "She used me to help her look first for the bronze gem, and then the amulet itself."

"What a *fascinating* story," Jack said, pretending to stifle a yawn. "Let me give you a hint, though, for future storytelling endeavors: show, don't tell. Stick to the facts. Your silver gem became Silverback's silver gem, and you got shanghaied by Madame Minuit. That just about sums it up?"

"Excuse me for being thorough. As I'm quickly learning, that's not really par for the course around here," Tim said sarcastically.

Jack held his hand up and suddenly looked serious.

"The one thing your story *does* prove is that this gem is connected to *this* medallion, the medallion is connected with Silverback, and Silverback is connected to Madame Minuit—how else would she have known to come for you?" Jack said. "Now," he continued, "there's only one thing left to do. . . ."

He took the silver gem and fitted it into the medallion.

CHAPTER TEN

$\mathcal{I}$f Jack was expecting a puff of smoke, a clap of thunder, or a shimmering curtain of magical sparks, he was sorely disappointed. The silver gem fit very neatly into its socket and clicked into place without a hitch. Once in, it looked like it had always been a part of the medallion.

Jack picked up the medallion and tapped it ceremoniously on the table. After all, when the bronze gem had been set into the medallion, all that was required was a light tap, and the object that was hit would turn to metal. Like his tooth, the ship, the city of New Orleans . . .

But this time, nothing happened.

Jean, Tumen, Fitzwilliam, and Tim stared at Jack dubiously. He tapped the medallion again—a little harder this time. Still nothing happened.

He looked at the medallion, puzzled, but Jack would rather be hanged than appear weak in front of Fitzwilliam and the others. "These things don't always work on the first try," he said cheerfully.

Just then, the door to the cabin flew open and Captain Laura Smith stood there, glaring at them. The five boys had been too engrossed in the medallion and Tim's story to notice the end of the fight between Arabella and her mom. It was obvious that Laura hadn't won. She looked to be in a right foul mood.

"How *dare* you enter my private chambers!" she cried. "Roaming about as if the *Fleur* was your own . . . personal . . ." she struggled for a word. "*SHIP!*" she finally said. Seeing Jack fight back a smile made her even angrier. "Captain Sparrow—I want you and your crew off my ship at once!"

"You, Madam Captain, are just as hotheaded as your daughter," Jack said with great admiration. With his left hand he swiftly and discreetly pulled the medallion off the table and slipped it into his pocket. The captain never noticed. She was too busy glowering. "And I would like to point out— just for the logbooks, as it were—" Jack continued, "that not only will I *gladly* disembark your invisible ship, but I never wanted to come aboard it in the first place. You and your mutinous crew forced us—*magicked* us—aboard, in fact. Against our will."

Jack marched dramatically past her, making a great show of climbing up the ladder through the hatch. Jean, Tumen, Tim, and Fitzwilliam followed suit, also with exaggerated care.

Captain Smith just growled and followed them closely, as if she were afraid they would steal something on the way out. Jack considered taking one of the semipreserved fish that sat in a barrel on deck, just to make a point. But he figured it wouldn't smell very good in his pocket.

Jean and Tumen rushed about the deck, untying the lines that held the *Barnacle* to the side of the *Fleur*. Tim watched them carefully and helped where he could. Arabella just stood defiantly. Her arms were crossed and her eyes were like loaded cannons. On second thought, maybe neither mother *nor* daughter won that fight.

A gull cried overhead and Jack grinned, taking a big gulp of air. This little hiccup in his adventure was almost over. Soon the *Barnacle* would be sailing on its own again, back to the Yucatán. And after that . . . well, just about anywhere they pleased. The ocean was his.

Captain Laura Smith watched their preparations to leave while discussing her own plans with Mr. Reece.

With a sudden burst of maturity, Jack decided he would be big about things. For good or ill, Laura *was* Arabella's mother. Even if she was a blasted pirate. Without her, the *Barnacle* would not have a first mate.

Feeling very charitable, Jack approached Captain Laura Smith, and gave her a fancy bow. Then he put out his hand. Looking at him suspiciously, the captain took it.

"Very nice to make your acquaintance,

Captain Smith," he said gallantly. "Perhaps we shall see each other again someday about the Caribbean."

Though he sorely hoped not.

It was obvious that Arabella's mother was thinking the same thing.

"Likewise," she lied.

"So," Jack said casually, looking from Laura to Mr. Reece, "what did you finally decide to do about your mutinous crew?"

"One by one, they will be brought before the captain and asked to swear allegiance," Mr. Reece said. "Those who don't will be immediately thrown overboard."

Jack laughed, then looked at Laura to see if this was at all a joke. He gulped when he saw the severe look in her eyes. She was dead serious. In this respect, at least, the mother and daughter were different. For all her bluster, Arabella would never have been so cold about hurting people, even pirates.

Jean, Tumen, Fitzwilliam, and Tim (and Constance) took their leave and boarded the *Barnacle*. Jack saluted and followed suit, leaving Arabella alone to say her final good-byes to her mother.

"So you have chosen to leave," her mother said grimly. "We were just reunited, and now you're going off with that insane captain and crew of yours."

Arabella shrugged. "I need some time to think about this. About you. I wish things could be different, but seeing you suddenly alive . . . knowing you were alive all these years . . . as a *pirate* . . . I'm angry, and confused . . . and *hurt* . . . and confused. I don't know what to tell you."

"Then let me make things a little easier for you," her mother offered, her smile softening. Then she nodded to Mr. Reece.

The first mate lunged forward and unsheathed his cutlass. With a sharp *crack* he brought it down on the last line that tied the *Barnacle* to the *Fleur*.

"No!" Jack cried out.

The *Barnacle* began to drift away. Within moments, the *Fleur*, with its magical sails unfurled, began to grow hazy and dim. In less than a minute, it was completely invisible.

Arabella was gone.

CHAPTER ELEVEN

*T*he crew of the *Barnacle* watched in bewilderment as they drifted from where the *Fleur de la Mort* once was. By squinting a little, Jack could just make out the water parting and the foam rising from where the ship should have been. It was heading north.

"Well," Jean said, speaking for everyone, "what shall we do now?"

"We *should* go back to Tumen's village and return the medallion to his great-grand-father," Jean pointed out. But he really didn't like the idea of Arabella being hauled off by her pirate mother.

"That would be the most reasonable course of action," Fitzwilliam agreed. "We made a promise. We owe a debt."

"Reasonable? Ha!" Jack laughed. "What we do next is *incredibly* obvious: we sail to New Orleans as well!"

Everyone looked at him questioningly.

"Everything is converging there," Jack pointed out. "Arabella, Silverback and Louis, Madame Minuit, who is after the medallion and knows everything about it—"

"Are you mad?" Fitzwilliam demanded. "Does finding out the true power of the medallion mean so much to you that you're willing to break a promise to Tumen?"

"It's not about the medallion, Lord Dolton Pennywhipple the *Third*. Did you not hear the first part of what I said?" Jack growled, rounding on Fitzwilliam. "Or do you want us just to abandon our first mate?"

Jack then turned to Tumen. "I have no intention of breaking any promise. We *will* return to your village. But if we don't go after Arabella now, we may never get her back. Unless you can think of some other way of tracking an invisible ship around the Caribbean. Savvy?"

"Is that really your decision, Jack?" Fitzwilliam demanded. "Arabella is finally reunited with her mother, who she has missed all these years. Understandably, she is quite confused right now . . . but she may choose to stay with her, once she gets her feelings sorted out."

"Which is *fine*," Jack said, throwing his arms up in the air, "if we knew Arabella happily *chose* to go along with her mum. But that stubborn woman-pirate *stole* her. You all heard Arabella—she wanted to stay with us! And the way they were fighting didn't make it sound as though they were going to make up any time soon. If we rescue Arabella and she chooses of her own free will to stay with that wretched captain, then she can go."

Jean, Tumen, and Tim nodded thoughtfully at this. At some point, each had had his whole life determined by someone else's choice. All three of them felt very strongly about Arabella's freedom to choose her own life.

"'Her own free will?'" Fitzwilliam asked. "She is just a teenager. Now that her mother is back in the picture, should it not be Laura Smith who has the final say on where her daughter lives and with whom?"

"Oh, I'm sorry, I completely *forgot*," Jack said with great sarcasm. "You're absolutely right, Fitzwilliam P. Dalton the *Third*.

Although, come to think of it, I'm pretty certain Fitzwilliam P. Dalton the *Second* probably wouldn't want his precious heir sailing around the Caribbean with the fugitive Jack Sparrow aboard the mighty *Barnacle*."

"Fugitive?" Tumen whispered to Jean. "I thought he told Arabella he was a stowaway."*

Jean shrugged. It was a mystery, but somehow not surprising coming from their mysterious and dramatic captain.

"You know I'm right," Jack prodded the nobleman's son.

Fitzwilliam turned beet red.

"I think you're supposed to say *touché*," Jack said generously, with a little bow.

"So, perhaps you have a point," the aristocrat admitted through gritted teeth.

* Back in Vol. 1 *The Coming Storm*

Jack grinned. He loved winning.

Jean frowned, noticing something. The way the bright sunlight reflected off of Jack's teeth. He leaned forward to get a better look.

Jack was surprised by this. "What's the matter, then—spinach in me teeth, mate?"

"*Écoutez*—look at this," Jean said, tapping Tumen on the shoulder.

Tumen stuck his face into Jack's as well. He frowned.

Intrigued, Tim and Fitzwilliam joined in, coming way too close for Jack's comfort. But when Constance jumped up onto Jean's shoulder and also peered down, breathing her terrible, catty breath in his face, he decided he'd had enough.

"Ah, mind stepping out of my personal space? Thank you," Jack said nervously, trying to back away.

But Jean grabbed him on one side and Tumen on the other.

"Here, this will help," Fitzwilliam said, reaching into his jacket. He pulled out a little pocket mirror, a slightly concave one. He carefully held it over his head, turning it to focus the rays of the sun onto Jack's teeth. Jean and Tumen held their captain tightly, not letting him look away.

"This is mutiny," Jack said, but with his mouth forced open it sounded like *issss issss oootinny*.

"*Oui*," Jean said, ignoring him. "It's silver."

"What?" Jack demanded, shaking himself loose. Tumen and Jean let him go. Fitzwilliam handed him the mirror.

"Your tooth. The bronze one," Fitzwilliam explained. "It is now silver."

Jack took the mirror and pointed it at his mouth, pulling his lips back. They were right. The dull goldish tooth was now a mercury-shiny silver one. He ran his tongue over it. Yep, tasted like silver, too.

"Well, I'll be," Jack said thoughtfully. "I wonder if that means that—"

Whatever he thought, it was interrupted by another set of blank, astonished faces from his crew. They weren't looking at him, though. They were looking over his shoulder.

"What is it *now*?" Jack demanded, irritated. "What could possibly be more fascinating than my silvery new tooth?"

Tumen just pointed wordlessly behind him. Jack slowly turned around, by now well used to the horrible and unexpected things the sea could produce. Monsters, sirens, half-pickled fish, ships made out of bronze . . .

And actually, it *was* a ship made out of metal. The same one Jack and the crew had sailed past a week before, in fact. The same ship that started this whole adventure—the one that had been turned to bronze, and was surrounded by bronze water.* More of the metal "water" had rusted and broken off from around it, but that wasn't the biggest difference.

It was now entirely silver.

Bright, shiny silver—so bright in fact that it was impossible to look at directly. The planks and portholes were like mirrors, the ropes like massive silver chains. It looked like something out of legend, something gods would ride in.

"As I was saying," Jack continued, trying not to be awed by the sight, "methinks the medallion works after all. . . ."

"Just not in the way we expected," Fitzwilliam finished.

"Everything that was turned into bronze

* For the full story, see Vol. 5, *The Age of Bronze*

is now turned into silver," Tim said, thinking out loud and nodding.

"If Bell were here she could probably give us some long-winded scientific or historical or magical explanation," Jack said.

Fitzwilliam didn't have a snooty answer this time. He looked at the deck. She had only been gone a little while and already they were all missing her.

"*Nouvelle Orléans!*" Jean suddenly realized. "The city must have all turned to silver as well!"

"That settles it, then!" Jack said gleefully, grabbing the wheel and giving it a spin. "We're Silver City bound, crew, to rescue our first mate!"

And no one had any objections this time. Not even Fitzwilliam P. Dalton III.

Don't miss the next volume in the continuing adventures of Jack Sparrow and the crew of the mighty Barnacle!

City of Gold

Jack and the crew of the *Barnacle* set sail for New Orleans to find Arabella. But what they find instead is . . . well, you'll just need to read the next volume to find out. And it has a shocking ending you won't want to miss!